THIS BOOK BELONGS TO:

EMMA BLANUSA

Sandcastle

Mick Inkpen

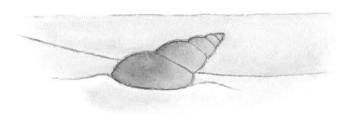

Hodder Children's Books

A division of Hodder Headline plc

Kipper was making
sandcastles.
It wasn't easy.
The first one wobbled
and fell over. The second
one crumbled at the corner.
But the third one
was just right.

Kipper made a big pile of sand and patted it smooth.

Then he dug, and piled, and patted some more. And this is what he made.

A seagull landed on
Kipper's castle.
It squawked and flew
away again.
'That's what I need!'
said Kipper.
'Something to
go on top!'

Kipper found some
seaweed and some
pebbles.

'No, they won't do,'
he said.

He found a shell.
It was pink and
pointy.

'Perfect!' he said.

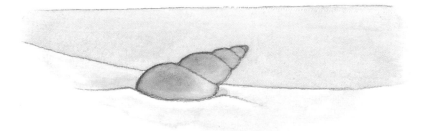

Kipper put the pink and pointy shell on his castle.

But the pink and pointy shell got up and walked away . . .

. . .there was a little crab inside!

So Kipper stopped
building his sandcastle.
He bought himself an
ice cream, and a sticky
lolly too!

While he was licking
the last bit of lolly,
an idea
popped into
his head.

He stuck the cone on the castle and the sticky lolly wrapper on the sticky lolly stick.

It looked even better than the pink and pointy shell. . .

. . .don't you think?

First published 1998
by Hodder Children's Books,
a division of Hodder Headline plc,
338 Euston Road, London NW1 3BH

Copyright © Mick Inkpen 1998

10 9 8 7 6 5 4 3 2 1

ISBN 0 340 71634 7

A catalogue record for this book
is available from the British Library.
The right of Mick Inkpen to be identitfied
as the author of this work
has been asserted by him.

Printed in Italy
Colour Reproduction by Dot Gradations, U.K.